BIRD OF PREY

A LANGSMITH SHIFTER SHORT

STELLA WILLIAMS

RAYA

Giving herself a shake, Raya fought off a moment of panic as gravity pushed her into the stiff back of her seat.

"Hate flying?"

The man sitting next to Raya gripped her hand in a show of support and, judging by the glint in his eye, attraction.

"This isn't flying, this is... I don't know what this is," she replied and pulled her hand away.

She closed her eyes. Raya cursed Sequoia for needing her and the little brat who shot her with his pellet gun while she'd been circling the park, ensuring she couldn't fly her preferred way. Most of all, she cursed Otto, the sexy bear shifter she hadn't been able to forget. Just the thought of the hulking, hairy beast made her body flush with arousal.

She should have never given in to the cocky furball. Who had ever heard of a bear and a bird shifter together, anyway? Not that bird shifters cared about cross-breeding. It was just rare that any actually mated outside of other bird shifter species. The most random pairing she had heard of was that of a Falcon and Finch.

What was she even thinking about? Mating the Bear? Impossible.

No matter how good he was in bed, no matter how her body instantly reacted to the man, their animals weren't compatible. Their worlds weren't compatible. She was a city bird, and he a country bear. She may be okay with the countryside for short visits, but no way could she make it her life.

The pull of gravity eased, and her stomach did a flip. She took a deep breath to stave off nausea—another poor decision on her part. Bile rose in her throat before she could react. Thankfully, the stranger had more experience with this sort of thing. He produced a paper bag, saving her clothing and the person in front of her.

The man rubbed her back. While she wished she could yell at the handsy man for taking liberties, it was helping, so she let it slide. The man pressed a button above them, and a flight attendant was there in seconds with extra paper bags and a bottle of water.

"Sorry," Raya muttered after carefully sipping the water.

"Happens all the time," the attendant said with a smile. "Just push this button if you need anything else."

The kind attendant indicated the button Raya's seatmate had pressed before she took off down the aisle.

"Ugh, how do people do this?" Raya groaned, sitting back in her chair with her eyes closed.

"At least, it's a short flight," her seatmate offered.

"I guess."

Raya felt the guy's hand inching close to hers again. She did not understand why this guy thought he could touch her so casually, but she wouldn't lie about not being entirely bothered by it. Raya opened her eyes and really studied the man beside her. She couldn't quite place why, but she felt like she knew him somehow.

He had short black hair and olive skin that made his green eyes stand out like emeralds. His sharp nose and jawline gave him a hawkish appearance, and that's when Raya recognized him.

"Hawkward?"

He frowned at her before shaking his head and letting his face fall into a natural smile.

"No one has called me that in ages. Please, I prefer Ward."

Raya blanched and nodded.

"Right, Ward. I'm sorry. It's just, I never thought, well..."

She barely got the words out as embarrassment rushed through her.

"It's quite alright. It's been a long time, Raya."

"But why are you flying... commercial?"

She couldn't help but ask. Ward and his family had once lived in the city. They'd been friends until puberty and peer pressure drove them apart. He'd been a late bloomer, and Raya had been an asshole like all the others at school. Then one day, they were gone. His entire family left without a word, and no one knew what happened. She knew he was a hawk but not his specific form because he hadn't yet had his first shift when she knew him.

"Flying under the radar, so to speak. I'm just here for a friendly visit and didn't want to deal with the drama that alternate travel would have caused."

He was cagey, but as they were surrounded by humans, he couldn't exactly be truthful. She did her best to read between the lines. Ward didn't look like he was hard up for money. Now that she knew who he was, it was easier to detect what caused her reaction to him. He was an Alpha; flying as his Hawk would have required him to extend the customary courtesies while traveling through another Alpha's territory. It could have easily added days, if not months, to his travel plans. Still, it felt like he hid something.

"Friendly visit?"

"Yes, my dear friend Tyr Greywulf."

"Interesting," Raya said, pretending she had no idea what he was talking about.

It was stupid, but Raya couldn't shake the feeling that there was more to this story. Especially since Sequoia had insisted on handling Raya's travel plans. She wouldn't put it past her happily mated best friend to attempt to match make for her, even amid pack drama. To be honest, Ward wouldn't be such a poor catch. They had been friends

once; he was now an Alpha, and he was also
a Hawk shifter. If mated, they could fly the
world together and have little bird of prey
babies.

That made her burst into a fit of laughter. Alpha or not. Hawk had always been too
conservative for her tastes.

"What's so funny?"

The confusion was clear as day on his
face.

"Nothing, I just remembered this funny
meme I saw," she lied.

He frowned but shrugged.

"Well, I am glad you are laughing now
instead of expelling your stomach into a
plastic bag."

Her laughter halted at the reminder of
her earlier state. Even if matchmaking had
been Sequoia's plan, no way would Ward
be interested in her when she couldn't even
handle a two-hour flight. He was obviously
used to traveling by human means of transportation. She couldn't picture plane rides
ever being a constant in her life. She turned
to look out the window. The familiar blue
of the sky and fluffy white clouds should
have helped ease her mind. Instead, it only

cemented how wrong this felt. Seeing them but not feeling them flowing through her feathers like silk over her human skin. It was a caress like no other.

An image of large, thick fingers roaming over the curve of her hip before dipping into her core flashed in her mind. Heat filled her as she let the memory play out instead of forcing it away. She closed her eyes, and for a moment, she could almost feel the coarse hair that covered Otto's chest and thighs rubbing against her skin, tickling and chaffing in all the right places. The sharp jolt of the plane as it hit a patch of turbulence stole her joy and caused her stomach to lurch once again.

Ward was right there with a new paper bag. Thankfully, she held it together this time. She smiled weakly at Ward before waving away his help with her uninjured arm. He made small talk with her, helping to pass the time until they landed.

"I guess this is where we say good-bye?" There was a glint in Ward's eyes as he spoke.

Raya shook her head and chuckled.

"See you later, Hawkward," she teased

before walking away after deplaning.

She knew he watched her go and couldn't resist exaggerating the swing of her hips as she walked away. Ward may not have been a viable candidate for a mate, but that didn't mean she couldn't have some fun with him during her stay.

OTTO

Otto forced his hands to his sides as he watched Raya flirt with Ward Buteo. He'd practically had to beg Sequoia to let him pick Raya up from the airport alone. A few moments to see if the spark was as strong as he remembered. Only to end up harangued into greeting both bird shifters out of duty.

Of course, Raya would be attracted to Buteo. He was an Alpha bird shifter in charge of one of the wealthiest and most influential flocks in all of Europe. Not to mention the owner of a large vineyard in the Italian countryside. Otto had noth-ing against Buteo, except the way the man leered after his mate.

Mate.

There was that word again. Otto clenched his fist tighter, using the burning sting of his nails in his palm to keep his bear at bay. A few passionate nights didn't a mate make, especially when she left you high and dry without a word as soon as the party was over. If things hadn't been so crazy with his Sleuth, he would have hightailed it to the city to make her his months ago. Otto always found it a little weird that Bears were a Sleuth instead of a pack. There was nothing detectivelike about bears.

Raya was too busy switching her hips for the other male to notice she was about to run into a discarded luggage cart. With a low growl, Otto moved quickly across the pavement, swooping her into his arms before she fell embarrassingly to her knees.

"You should watch where you're going," he ground out.

He felt Raya tense, ready for battle mode, but she looked up and saw him. Her mouth fell open in surprise before she quickly shut it and pushed out of his arms.

"What are you doing here?" she demanded.

"Sequoia sent me," he said.

Raya raised an eyebrow at him and crossed her arms over her chest.

"Why the hell would she do that?"

"Is there a problem here?" Ward asked, standing too close to Raya for Otto's comfort.

His bear bristled. He could feel the tingling under his skin, the bear ready to surface and challenge the other shifter over its mate.

RAYA

Raya saw the tick in Otto's jaw as he fought to reign in his bear. It should have bothered her that he was ready to go all *agro* over her, but it was super fucking hot. She couldn't resist playing with the fire she saw dancing in his eyes.

She turned to Ward and placed her hand on his chest. She leaned forward and put on her best damsel in distress face.

"No problem, just an old acquaintance. Would you like to ride with me? It seems we are headed in the same direction." She batted her eyelashes for added effect.

Ward smiled at her and nodded.

"Normally, I would love to, but I don't know who Tyr sent to pick me up. It would be ungracious of me to change plans without notifying him first."

Otto spoke then.

"Tyr sent me." His tone was much calmer than before.

Raya spun around to find Otto smirking at them both. It wasn't a friendly smirk either. He was pissed, and Raya had no intention of being in the middle of this Alpha male pissing contest for the next hour. The flight had been taxing enough. She pulled out her phone and dialed Sequoia, but Otto took the phone from her hand before Sequoia answered.

"Hey, Coy! I just wanted you to know we are on our way." He hung up her phone, and Raya snatched her phone back.

"How dare you," she began, but Otto pulled her into his arms and kissed her.

She could protest all she wanted, but as soon as his lips touched hers, Raya knew she was in trouble. Her body immediately responded, and she wrapped her arms around his neck and wished they were somewhere more private. Just when she was about to really lose herself in him, Otto pulled away.

"I'll do whatever I please. You're in my territory now, sweetheart," he said and pulled her toward the parking lot.

"Not for long," she grumbled.

Raya glanced back at Ward, who shook his head, disgust written on his face as she was dragged away by Otto. He kept a respectful distance all the way to the truck. So much for distracting herself with Ward. She should have known something like this would happen. Otto was Tyr's best friend, after all. She'd just hoped she could avoid him for most of her visit. She promised herself the night at the Shifter Gathering would be the last, and she meant to keep that promise.

At the last moment, Raya pulled out of Otto's grasp.

"You boys enjoy the ride. I am sure you have plenty of business you need to discuss. I'll just grab a rental like I originally planned." She walked away quickly before either male could protest. Thankfully, neither followed as she made her way back into the airport. Raya added dodging Otto to her list of plans for her stay.

OTTO

"Stubborn woman," Otto grumbled before turning a grin to Ward.

The other Alpha shrugged and climbed into the passenger seat. Otto gave Raya's retreating form one last look before jogging around to the driver's side.

"I'm so sorry about my behavior. That woman drives me mad," Otto said as he pulled off.

Ward nodded and pulled out his phone.

"Do you know what's going on and why I am here?" Ward asked.

Otto snorted, not liking the man's tone. It wasn't uncommon for two Alphas near each other to be tense with one another, but Otto knew it wasn't just their Alpha status at odds. Ward wanted what was his. He wanted Raya, and Otto would be damned if he gave the man the slightest chance to come between him and his mate.

"I'm not clear on the details, but I know

that Langsmith is in trouble. You being here only confirms my suspicions of how much trouble," Otto replied.

Ward nodded again. He was apparently a man of few words, or he, like Otto, wasn't interested in being all buddy-buddy with his competition. For the rest of the drive, both men stayed silent. Ward stared at his phone while Otto focused on the road and his plans to get Raya alone. She was injured, and it killed him not to be taking care of her. Just as it filled him with murderous rage at whoever had hurt her.

Otto, occupied with thoughts of his bear dismembering the imaginary perpetrator, almost missed the turnoff to the entrance of the Langsmith Pack Compound. He pulled up short to the gate and stopped the truck. He usually called Tyr and the gates would open for him. Still, Otto wasn't keen on spending another minute alone with the dismissive bird next to him.

"It's not a far walk. Cars are discouraged past this point," Otto said.

Ward didn't look pleased with the idea of trekking up the muddy road in his clean white sneakers, but it was the man's own

fault. Who wore white sneakers to a rural
Shifter compound? Still, Ward was out of
Otto's truck and heading down the path in a
matter of seconds. Otto didn't linger to see
him clear the first bend. Instead, he pulled
onto the road and headed home. He needed
a minute to regroup before he did anything
else that afternoon.

Tyr would let him know if there was
anything else he needed. Besides, Otto had
his own people to manage. The Surge, as Tyr
and Sequoia called it, had reached as far as
his territory. It hadn't hit his Sleuth as hard.
Still, it definitely made things interesting
for the teens who had shifted earlier than
excepted. He had a whole new group of cubs
to train.

Speaking of training, Otto knew grabbing a few treats for the new bears on his
way home would go over well. A few sugary
snacks were the perfect way to end a hard
day's training. Otto pulled into the last gas
station before his place to pick up a few
things. As he paid for a horde of twinkies,
cupcakes, and sugar bombs, none other than
Raya came striding in.

She narrowed her eyes at him.

"Are you stalking me now?"

Otto frowned and finished paying for his things.

"This is the only gas station between my place and Langsmith. I like you a lot, Raya, but stalking is too far even for me," he said.

Otto smiled at the attendant and left the shop area, but once in his truck, he couldn't go. Not until he knew she was safely back in her rental. The gas station attendant was a young kid and posed no threat to her, but the group of bikers out front gave him something to worry about. Sure enough, as she exited the shop, two bikers approached her.

Her stance was defensive, and he noticed her hand going into her purse. He was out of the truck and by her side before she could draw whatever weapon she had. The bikers immediately backed off when confronted by Otto's massive frame. That, and Otto had run into conflict with this particular group before. They knew even with their numbers, he could tear them all to shreds.

"I could have handled them," Raya grumbled behind him.

Her words set off something inside of him. There was nothing he could have done to stop what was about to happen. Sweeping her into his arms, he kissed her until she melted against him.

"Let's get out of here," Otto said during a forced pause for air.

Raya's eyes danced with arousal as she pressed herself close to him.

"I saw a hotel just up the road."

That was the last place Otto had in mind, but she was already sliding into her rental car. He opened his mouth to suggest she follow him to his home, but she took off, and he had no choice but to follow. Shaking his head, Otto knew precisely where this was going to end up. He just hoped he could avoid getting burned by the one woman who held the power to override his stubborn streak.

RAYA

Raya kept her hands close to her body as Otto hustled her to the motel room he'd rented. She'd tried desperately to talk herself out of it on the short trip over, but her body wasn't having it. Ever since the moment Raya laid eyes on the behemoth of a man, she could count on one hand how many times her brain had overruled her libido. This rendezvous was inevitable. It was better she have her fill and move along.

Otto was quick with the door, spinning her inside and pressing her against the sticky red finish as it slammed shut. His mouth claimed Raya's in a kiss so gentle she almost didn't recognize the man in front of her. His eyes glowed with emotions she didn't dare dwell upon. She closed her eyes, focusing on the rough way Otto palmed her breast. He squeezed her to just the slightest bit of pain before releasing her and letting his thumb travel over her taut nipples. She moaned, her back arching away from the door and closer to his touch.

OTTO

This was all wrong and perfectly right all at once. Otto wanted to slow things down, to take his time. Show Raya he knew how to worship her body just as well as he could manhandle it the way she liked. Taking her against the door of a motel wasn't the most romantic thing Otto could have done. Hell, he should have been more patient and brought her back to his home, some place nicer and most definitely cleaner. Otto's shifter senses could pick up on about six different dubious scent trails in the room, but he focused on only one. The scent of his mate's arousal pooling between her legs.

With a growl, he pulled her from the door and onto the bed. Stripping off the scrap of fabric she called pants, he sank between her legs. Mouth watering, he nuzzled her bare flesh. Covering his face and mouth with her intoxicating musk before allowing himself the first sip of her sweet nectar. His bear purred like a damn kitten as he lapped at her.

Raya's soft mewling sounded like music to his ears as he licked and suckled her core. He could never get enough of this. Never get enough of her. *Mate*. Otto was too far gone to worry about his bear's premature declarations. Raya would be his mate, just not now. It needed to be her choice too. He fought the urge to mark her as he continued to pleasure her. Tiny nails pricked the skin of his shoulders as she gripped them, holding him in place. Her hips moved frantically against his tongue. He was submerged in her core and loved every moment of her pleasure as if it were his own.

Mine!

Otto couldn't be sure if it was his bear jumping the gun again or his own roaring bellow as both were drowned out by Raya's earsplitting cry of release. She was his alright, and after tonight, maybe she would understand it, too.

RAYA

Heavy snoring rang out from the giant male sprawled naked on the motel bed. Raya gave the hairy behemoth a final once-over while she wiggled into her pants.

"This is the last time," she muttered to herself.

Even as she said the words, she knew they were a lie. The last time was supposed to be the last time. Shaking her head, Raya left the room. Slinging her purse over her good shoulder, she made the walk of shame back to her rental car before pulling out her phone. She sent a quick text to her best friend, Sequoia.

Coy! I'm almost at your place! Can't wait to see you!

Raya wasn't surprised that her best friend answered almost immediately. Sequoia had turned into quite the morning person since moving into the wilderness with her mate, Tyr.

*No worries! Take your time. *winky face**

Raya snorted and tossed her phone on the passenger seat. Apparently, she wasn't the only one with a hot shifter in her bed problem. Her body yearned for her to go back and wake the sleeping bear shifter in the hotel room, but common sense made her put the car in gear and head downtown. Langsmith, California was nothing like home, but they at least had a decent coffee shop or two.

She would grab a pastry and a break from her raging hormones before joining Coy to deal with whatever trouble Tyr had gotten them into this time. Coy had been vague on the phone about what exactly had happened. Still, the supernatural community was small and full of nosey gossips. Shifters especially, so Raya knew she was in for a fight by coming here. In just a few more days, she'd have full use of her arm again, and when that happened, nothing would be able to touch her.

The Langsmith area was one of the few cities where supernaturals intermingled freely. It was a hotspot of energy that drew

Vampires, shifters, and all sorts of magical beings to the area. Even the annual Shifter Gathering was held in the Devil Wolf Mountains not far from Langsmith. Speaking of the Shifter Gathering, Raya's typically laid-back parents had lost their minds ever since Sequoia had come back mated and not Raya. It seemed her parents' wishes for grandkids were more pressing than her need for freedom.

At the thought of being tied down, Raya felt tiny feathers pressing at her skin. Her Eagle wasn't a fan of the idea either. At least, when it came to thoughts of any male other than the one she knew better than to want. Otto Thorburn of West Cliff was the last shifter male she should have been attracted to; he was her complete opposite. He was also a bear shifter, and everyone knew bears only mated with other bears.

OTTO

Otto woke the moment the door slammed shut. Grunting, he shot to a seated position, his arm reaching out to protect his mate only to find cool sheets instead of warm female flesh.

"Shit!"

He had meant to be a gentleman. To get up early and surprise Raya with breakfast in bed and all that. But his Bear still hadn't shaken its hibernation lethargy yet. That meant he'd slept like the dead and likely kept her up all night snoring like the giant bear he was. It also meant he'd missed his chance to stake his claim on the elusive bird shifter, his true mate.

Otto's phone buzzed somewhere in the room. He hopped up and went on a search. He hadn't cared where his clothes ended up when they came in. It had been all about getting Raya's tiny little body naked and under his as quickly as possible. When he'd run into her at the gas station, he'd meant to invite her to dinner. Yet, his need to claim his mate had overridden any thoughts of chivalry, and they had grabbed a room in the shitty roadside motel next door. His mate deserved better than a seedy motel screwing.

His pants were tossed over the corner of the dresser, but his phone wasn't in his pants pocket. The buzzing had stopped, so he no longer had that to help him on his search. He found his boxers on the other side of the room and slid them on before going to retrieve his pants. As much as Otto wanted to lay naked in wait of his mate, there was business he couldn't put aside.

Tyr had called for his help in managing the fallout of the Aura-Vampire skirmishes in Langsmith. As the Alpha of his own pack in the mountains just north of Langsmith, it was his job to make sure the city drama stayed far away from his Sleuth. It seemed his friendship with Tyr had drawn him and his Sleuth further into the city and into the fight. It wasn't the shifter way, and it sure as hell wasn't the bear shifter way to interfere in other people's business, but Tyr was a dear friend. If Vampires and the Aura brought too much attention to the supernatural world, it was bad business for everyone—even those on the outskirts like Otto.

His phone buzzed again. He found it wedged between the nightstand and the bed, but his shirt was nowhere to be found. All he could see was the torn remains of the silk blouse Raya had worn. A smile stretched across his face as he realized she must have snagged his shirt to wear. The thought of her wrapped in something he owned, carrying his scent with her for the rest of the day, made his bear rumble with contentment. Especially knowing it would be a signal to any shifter near her that she was spoken for.

Checking the screen, Otto realized he needed to snap out of the mating fog. Not only had Tyr called him, but the head of the Shifter Council's number flashed across his screen.

"Yes, sir?" he answered.

"Get your ass to Langsmith. We have a situation," Shifter Elder Gary snapped before hanging up.

Cursing, Otto headed to his truck shirtless. He had a change of clothes in the back seat, as any responsible shifter did, but he'd grab a shirt when he got into pack territory. For now, he booked it toward Langsmith Pack Territory. The drive wasn't long, and it gave him a chance to gather his thoughts.

Otto hopped out of his truck just outside of Langsmith Compound and prepared for the trek into the woods. The wolves were more social than Otto's bears, but that didn't mean they made it easy to get to their compound. There was only one vehicle accessible road, and it was blocked by a big steel gate. There was a small turn off where visitors could park and walk-in, but mostly, uninvited visitors were discouraged. The fact that more of the Shifter Council had dropped in without notifying Tyr first wasn't good. The entire Shifter Council only got involved when things really hit the fan.

RAYA

"I really hate the patriarchy of pack politics," Sequoia grumbled, plopping down in the seat across from Raya.

Raya had settled in with her cappuccino when Sequoia called demanding to know where she was and complaining about the Shifter Council's unannounced visit.

"You choose an Alpha mate, you choose pack politics," Raya chuckled.

She shouldn't have found humor in her friend's predicament, but Raya always strove to find the upside of things. Even when it was a deeply troubling event. Something must have been horribly wrong if the Shifter Council involved itself in a local pack's business.

"So, what exactly did you call me here for? I mean, I am glad to visit any time, but you sounded scared when we last talked."

Sequoia glanced around the coffee shop and leaned closer.

"Can we talk about that later?"

Her eyes shifted around the room again. Raya followed her gaze and noted they had somewhat of an audience.

"Sure. How's mated life?"

Sequoia smiled and sat back.

"It's great. Tyr is everything I could ever want in a mate. It's the adjustment to pack life that's jarring for me. I mean, I've never had so much family," Sequoia said.

Raya laughed.

"You mean, so many people all in your business. Tell me. How many people are betting on when you'll be with a pup?"

Sequoia rolled her eyes.

"Far too many. I mean, I love Tyr and want to have kids with him someday, just not so soon. I mean, we are already taking care of Sarah, and being the wife of the Alpha means I'm kind of mom to everyone, anyway."

"How is Sarah doing? She still a feral little scamp?"

"She's adjusting to the pack life. She's finally acting her age, at least."

Raya smirked.

"That's good."

Sequoia's eyes twinkled with mischief before she opened her mouth to speak again.

"So, are you and Otto finally giving it a go?"

With a snort, Raya set down her coffee before she spilled it everywhere from laughing so hard.

"Hardly, we ran into each other at the gas station is all."

"At the gas station, huh? Is that some new slang for screwing each other's brains out? You know I'm a wolf, right? Even without my heightened senses, you are fucking glowing with contentment, and you're wearing the shirt Tyr and I gave him for Christmas. Flannel looks good on you, by the way."

"Everything looks good on me. So what if we screw around? We're just having fun."

Sequoia pegged her with a stern look before sighing.

"Look, I get that you have this freedom is life thing going, but Otto is the last man who would try to clip your wings. Just give it a real shot. I love you both, and I really think you two make a great pair."

"Oh, spare me the mating drama. Like I said, we are both just having fun. I'm not ruling out anything more, but come on, Coy. You and I both know, even if we felt the mating pull for each other. He's a bear, and I'm a bird. It would never work."

"You never know unless you try, but fine, I won't push. Just be aware that you will stay with Otto's Sleuth for this trip. It isn't exactly safe in Langsmith and with the Shifter Council in town, our extra rooms are full up."

Raya frowned.

"Seriously?"

"Sorry." Sequoia shrugged.

"It's not a problem. I can be on my best behavior in front of Otto's Sleuth."

"Good, then it's settled. You'll have dinner with us and ride back with Otto. It's best if he brings you into his territory. His Sleuth can be aggressive toward strangers."

"Of course."

Raya was totally not okay with the idea of being in Otto's territory. Especially when that meant she would be subject to the female bears who no doubt sought the affection of their bachelor Alpha. She suddenly felt uncomfortable in his shirt where before it had provided a sense of comfort.

"Mind if we do a little shopping?"

Sequoia smiled.

"Not at all. Mind if I call Sarah and see if she wants to join us? She is becoming quite the fashionista, and I have no idea how to guide her."

Raya grinned at that.

"Of course, I'll be glad to help her spread her fashion wings."

Within the hour, they had picked up Sarah and were on their way out of town to the nearest mall.

OTTO

Otto had known things were bad, but he didn't think it had reached the point for Council involvement. At least, not until he entered the meeting hall and saw not only the Shifter Council but a Vampire and an Aura in the Langsmith Pack Meeting Hall.

"You know, a heads up would have been nice," Otto said to Tyr after the outsiders had left and the Council was deliberating in private.

Tyr frowned and shook his head.

"Walk with me," he said.

Otto followed his friend far away from the meeting house and prying ears and eyes.

"Look, there is more going on than even the Council knows. I haven't exactly played neutral in things around here."

Otto snorted. He knew damn well Tyr was more involved than he had let on in the meeting. How else could bringing a Vampire and an Aura to meet the Shifter Council be explained?

"I figured. So, what's really going on?"

Tyr signaled for him to take a seat with him on a nearby stump.

"First, I don't want you to think I didn't trust you with the information I'm about to tell you. I honestly was trying to handle this without dragging anyone else into it."

"Understood."

"Ceres was real."

Otto's heart skipped a beat.

"Are you shitting me? Wait... *was* real? Does this have anything to with that weird surge?"

Tyr nodded.

"Long story short, Vampires were hunting Aura with the help of a corrupt Aura official. The Aura retaliated by killing a Vampire Council member, and now we have Aura refugees from Ceres and Vampires on our asses."

Otto waited for Tyr to say more, but after a moment realized that was all the explanation he was going to get.

"So, what does that have to do with shifters?"

Tyr ran a hand over his face.

"Vampires haven't just been hunting Aura. They've been taking shifters too. So, I started working with the Aura and a group of rogue Vamps to track down these supernatural trafficking centers. New relationship meant I couldn't just let shit go down and not help them out when the Vampires attacked."

Otto let out a heavy sigh.

"Shit."

"Yeah, shit."

"So now the Shifter Council is involved, and you're trying to play it straight while still helping them under the table."

"Exactly."

Otto eyed his friend, letting the gravity of the situation sink in.

"You know your pack is welcome in the mountains if things get too heated here."

Tyr smirked and shook his head.

"Thanks, I'll keep that in mind if it comes to that." A glint of mischief lit Tyr's eyes before he spoke again. "Speaking of, do you mind housing Raya for us? The Council's visit took up our available space."

Otto laughed.

"I wouldn't mind at all, bro. In fact, it

would be my pleasure."

"I figured."

Both men laughed, releasing some of the tension they held from the conversation before.

"Shit, man. Let's go for a run."

"You sure that's a good idea right now?"

"No, but all the stress I'm in right now, my wolf needs a stretch."

Without waiting for Otto's reply, Tyr stood and stripped out of his clothes. Tyr was already in wolf form by the time Otto had stripped to join him.

"Pesky canine," Otto growled in a partial shift as he tossed his shirt to the side. In minutes, they had both fully turned and headed off into the forest.

RAYA

Shopping turned out to be less fun than Raya expected. Although there was a mall, there wasn't much in either woman's style to be had. The only boon had been a cute lingerie boutique that Sarah had cringed and whined throughout Raya and Coy's shopping spree. Raya managed to snag a few things she reluctantly hoped a certain bear shifter would ruin sometime later this trip.

"I missed this," Coy blurted.

"Me too. I mean, minus the grumpy teen tag along." Raya nodded at Sarah, who narrowed her eyes at her.

"You didn't have to invite me," Sarah scowled.

Coy shot Raya a frustrated look before turning to face Sarah in the back seat.

"Raya's just teasing. We both enjoyed having you with us."

Raya smirked. It was strange hearing such a maternal tone from her one-time party girl friend.

"Sure, can you guys drop me off at the Youth Center? I've got stuff to do."

Raya thought nothing of the request, but Coy's huffy response was enough to raise Raya's hackles.

"I thought you weren't doing that anymore," Coy said.

"It's not for work, I actually have friends, you know," Sarah said before raising her phone to cover her face.

Raya glanced at Coy, who waved her hand in defeat.

"Fine. Raya, go back into town and take a right at the street before the café," Coy said.

Raya followed Coy's directions, and soon, they pulled up to a standard looking youth center complete with a run-down basketball court and colorful mural of a civil rights activist. Sarah barely waited for the car to come to a full stop. She jumped out the door and jogged to a group of teens hanging out by the dumpsters.

"You want to circle the block, make sure she isn't smoking or vaping?" Raya offered.

Coy shook her head.

"Sarah's a good kid. It's just the Vampires attacked the youth center a few weeks ago."

Raya's eyebrows lifted a good three inches in surprise.

"Seriously, and you let her go?"

"I know, I'm a terrible mother," Coy groaned.

Raya chuckled and circled the block, anyway. Sarah glared at them as they cruised by a second time, but it didn't seem like they had anything to worry about, so they headed to the local ice cream shop.

"So, it's been awful here?" Raya asked, looking over the community board filled with missing persons.

"Yeah, I mean, who'd have thought I would be in more danger here in the burbs than in the city?" Coy laughed.

"Me! Didn't you know that's where all the serial killers hang out?" Raya laughed, earning her disgruntled looks from some of the surrounding patrons.

Coy shushed at her and smacked her arm.

"Don't joke about that. It's still too fresh."

Raya sighed and paid for the two pints of ice cream they had ordered to-go.

"Alright, alright. Let's just get back to the compound so we can chill and chat in peace."

Coy nodded, but as they headed out the door, they ran into a group of young boys. The sun was already setting, and the tingling on the back of Raya's neck told her these weren't your run-of-the-mill teenage punks. Coy bristled and got closer to Raya, and the teens circled.

"Well, look what we've got here," one of the Vamps snarled.

They circled and attempted to back teh women into the nearby alley, but Coy and Raya knew better. Not just as shifters, but it was run-of-the-mill street smarts not to enter a dark ass alley when in a compromised position. There were four Vampires, not insurmountable odds if a fight was to be had. Still, with humans nearby, neither Coy nor Raya could shift without exposing themselves.

Cursing her still sore arm, Raya reached into her purse for her pepper spray, but she didn't need it. Suddenly, Sarah showed with her friends. Energy crackled in the air around them and made Raya's skin crawl. The Vampires turned their attention to the new arrivals, hissing and flashing fangs. One of Sarah's friends raised their hand, and the air seemed to wrap around it before moving forward in a wave that knocked the Vampires back.

"Get out of our territory," the boy said, more energy rolling off him and pushing the Vampires farther and farther back.

Eventually, the Vampire quartet turned and made a run for it.

"This isn't over," one of the Vampires yelled back at them.

As soon as the Vamps were out of sight, the boy lowered his arm and smiled. Sarah rushed forward and hugged both Raya and Sequoia close.

"Are you alright?"

"Yes, we're fine. Thank you," Coy said.

"That was..." Raya didn't even know how to describe it.

It wasn't her first time encountering an Aura, but it was the first she'd seen of them using their abilities. It was impressive and terrifying.

Nothing. Just doing our job to protect the community," Sarah's friend said before turning to leave.

"I'll be home by dinner," Sarah called and trailed after her friends.

Coy didn't relax until she and Raya were back in the car.

"Welcome to Langsmith," she muttered, and Raya laughed.

"Thanks."

OTTO

"You were what?" Tyr shouted as Sarah let slip the events from earlier that day.

The dinner plates and glassware rattled as his Alpha voice boomed through the room. Raya cringed, and Otto immediately pulled her to his side.

"It was fine. Me and the Resistance were nearby, and we dealt with it. Coy and Raya are safe," Sarah said.

"Thankfully, but I thought I told you not to hang out down there anymore."

Sarah frowned at him.

"So, I can't have friends now?"

Sarah stormed from the table, leaving an irate Tyr and a frustrated Coy behind.

"I gave her permission to hang out with them today," Coy said, and Tyr calmed a little.

The tension slowly eased out of the air as he reeled himself in, but Otto knew his best friend was not okay with the situation at all. Otto wasn't either. No shifter was okay with their mate being in danger, especially if they weren't there to protect them. Otto pulled Raya tighter to his side until she was practically in his lap.

"I think we should give them some privacy," Raya purred in his ear.

Otto didn't have to be told twice. He rose from the table, bringing Raya right along with him.

"It's going to be a drive out to my place. So, we'll just head out and see you tomorrow," Otto said.

He didn't wait for Tyr or Sequoia to acknowledge him. Instead, he wrapped his arm around Raya's waist and ushered her toward the door. Otto helped Raya into the passenger seat of his truck, his hand lingering on her ass.

"You know, just because I am going home with you, doesn't mean I'm "going home" with you," she said.

Otto's bear growled at the thought of her rejecting them, but Otto tamped it down.

"The choice to come to my bed has always been yours, Birdy."

"Don't call me Birdy."

"Tweety?"

"No!"

"Featherweight?"

"Definitely not. Raya is just fine, thank you."

"Birdy, it is."

Raya huffed and crossed her arms over her chest. Otto knew his eyes should have been on the road, but the way her folded arms cradled her ample bosom created a major distraction.

"Look, we've fooled around a bit. Our best friends are mated. I get your need for familiarity, but I want to make one thing clear. I gave up teddy bears years ago."

The tone of her voice seemed serious, but Otto could see her fighting a smile. Her luscious lips twitched, and a dimple appeared that reminded him of a honey-comb. His bear growled. Bears did love their honey. Otto shifted in his seat to relieve the pressure his dick put on the seam of his pants, but it was no use. His foot pressed harder on the gas. The speedometer inched well past the speed limit as he tried to make the trip home as short as safely possible. As

much as he wanted her, Otto would wait. He
would prefer to have her in a proper bed.
Not take her on the side of the road like an
animal.

RAYA

Raya turned to face out the window, hiding the smile on her face. Otto kept one hand firmly on her thigh. She kept her arms folded across her chest to hide her nipples that peaked under the thin fabric. Otto's musky scent filled the cabin of the truck. The ultimate aphrodisiac. She crossed and uncrossed her legs as arousal pooled between them. The world raced by the window, faster and faster, until all she saw was a blur of browns and greens.

Any sane shifter female would have welcomed the attention of an established Alpha, but not Raya. Especially knowing that meant she could never be his mate and live in the city as she preferred. As if sensing her inner turmoil, Otto's thumb brushed higher on her leg, dancing perilously close to her sensitive bud. Jeans were too hard to pull up with one functioning arm, so she had opted for loose-fitting harem pants. The thin fabric did nothing to shield her body from the heat of his touch. She bit her lip to keep from mewling as he stroked her.

She knew how this was going to end. Despite her protests, she wanted Otto, badly. She knew he wanted her, too. That was what made staying away so hard. They both knew what was going on between them couldn't be more than a fling. Neither of them had the willpower to stay out of each other's arms. If she had been smart, she would have insisted on driving herself to his place. Still, with the wariness of the Sleuth, it had been decided before dinner that riding with him was the best and safest choice.

At least, it would have been if it wasn't for the intense attraction they shared. Unable to help herself, Raya scooted closer to Otto on the bench seat. There was no denying the pheromones her body produced in her arousal. She clutched the dashboard, her talons bursting forth as she reached peak. She had never lost control of her Eagle like this, not even in her early transition stage.

She glanced at Otto, who cringed at the sight of his crushed dashboard but shifted to a smug smile as he felt the wetness seeping

through her pants. He coated his fingers
with her release and brought it to his mouth.
A low growl reverberated through him.
Raya's hand fell to his lap, feeling the bulge
at the seam of his pants—the truck swerving
a little on the road.

"Raya," Otto hissed in warning.

A smile tugged at her lips as she slid the
zipper of his fly down. Raya wiggled her slim
fingers into the opening. The truck jerked
to the left as she wrapped her hand around
him and freed him from the tangle of his
cotton boxers and jeans. It sprung free,
standing erect like a flagpole, the tip glis-
tened reflecting the glow of the dashboard
lights of the tiny beads of pre-cum that coated the bulbous head.

She teased the head with her thumb,
spreading his juices over the base. Otto
slammed on the breaks. Raya had been so
focused on teasing him that she hadn't realized he had veered off the main road. She
flew forward. Otto caught her with his arm
before hauling her into his lap.

"I was trying to get you to a bed first,
damn it," he cursed before crushing his
mouth to hers.

"Beds are overrated," Raya moaned, her hips grinding against his leg as she continued to stroke his shaft.

His hand slid up her shirt to cup her breast and thumb her taut nipple. His enormous hands made her feel so small and delicate. One snap of his thick fingers could break her in two, and that was both horrifying and sexy as fuck. Otto was a big teddy bear, but she knew he could also be a dangerous wild animal. Especially for her heart.

"Otto!" She gasped as he ground his hips against hers. The warm length of him slid against her, causing delicious friction that shot lightning rods of pleasure through her entire body. Her hips moved, matching his rhythm, ensuring the maximum amount of contact.

"That's it, love," he ground against her long and slow, "take what you need."

Her butt hit the steering wheel, making the horn go off, jarring her back to reality. She stilled and forced herself out of Otto's lap. Breathing heavily, they sat in silence.

"A bed it is then," Otto said before stuffing himself back into his pants.

Raya placed her hand on his arm before

he could put the car into drive again.

"We can't keep doing this," she said.

Otto's hand fell from the shifter, and he maneuvered his massive body until he faced her.

"Can't keep doing what, Raya?"

She bit her lip and tried to turn away from his piercing scrutiny, but he pulled her back into his lap.

"Talk to me, Birdy. What can't we do?"

Raya sighed and rested her head on his shoulder. It was safer than looking him in the eyes.

"This," she muttered.

She hated being such a coward that she couldn't put into words the way her heart and her Eagle felt about this man. About Otto. She was afraid if she said the words out loud, there would be no taking them back, that she could never walk away from him and live in peace. What if he didn't share her feelings? Hell, even if he did, his Sleuth would never accept her as one of them, and Raya wasn't sure she could commit to staying in one place for the rest of her life. She would never make him choose between her and his people.

OTTO

Otto waited patiently for Raya to elaborate on what the hell she was talking about. Of course, they could have sex. They had done it at least a hundred times before. Did Raya want more? Otto's heart swelled with the possibility. He'd never assumed she would see him as a potential mate without some convincing, but with the way she was acting now. So unsure, so cautious. He hated that he had anything to do with it.

Otto pushed Raya back until she was forced to look at him. Really look at him. The sadness in her eyes nearly undid him, but he didn't want to have this conversation here. In the cramped space of his truck where he couldn't see her properly. Couldn't express himself in the way he needed to.

"You're right, we can't do this. Not here."

He let her slide off his lap, and she crawled to the other side of the cab, putting as much distance between them as she could. His bear roared inside him, pissed that he was allowing their mate to feel any moment of uncertainty about where they stood. Not for the first time, Otto was glad he had firm control over his bear. Otherwise, Raya would be engulfed in a real-life bear hug.

The rest of the drive to his cabin was made in near silence. After a few minutes of not talking, Raya had reached over to turn the radio on. Making it clear she had no intention of discussing things further with him. Not that Otto knew what to say. Small talk didn't seem right, and he wanted her at his house before he laid himself and his heart at her feet.

At least, the drive wasn't much longer. On the private road that led to Otto's home, the forest became denser, blocking out the light of the moon. As a stray branch scratched the hood and sides of his truck, Otto made a mental note to cut back the overgrowth tomorrow. He would need manual labor to work out his frustration if she turned him away after he declared his love.

Raya gasped when they entered the

clearing the held the Sleuth Lodge and Otto's cabin. Bears were more solitary and needed their space. While most of the Sleuth preferred their bear forms and living in the wild, a few of the families with cubs liked more human comforts. They had their own cabins spread out across the property. Still, the lodge acted as both Sleuth headquarters, temporary housing for wilder bears, and storage, so it was built in a central location. As Alpha, it only made sense that Otto lived near where he did most of his business.

For Otto, it was just home, but he tried to imagine it through Raya's eyes. He remembered her teasing him about being a mountain man. She probably thought he lived in a cave or some stick hut. Seeing the grandness of the lodge was perhaps a shock to her. He just hoped she wouldn't be disappointed with his more modest abode. He rounded the large cabin and parked his truck by the garage.

"You live here?" Raya finally spoke.

"Not quite," Otto snorted.

He got out of the truck and ran around to help her out. It made him feel slightly better that she didn't refuse his help when he lifted her out of the truck, but she was quick to get back on her feet and put distance between them once she was out.

Otto grabbed her bag and motioned for her to follow him.

"You aren't taking me into the woods to kill me, are you?"

Otto whipped around to face her and was surprised to see the huge grin on her face.

"Joking, joking," she laughed.

Otto tried to relax. He was much too on edge for her jokes but it was best she attempted to ease the tension between them.

"My place is just behind the garage," he grumbled.

He hadn't realized he was walking too fast for her until he felt a slight breeze and heard the flapping of wings above him. He looked up to see the silhouette of an Eagle. He stopped and admired the grace of her dancing in the open night sky before she came and landed on his shoulder. Her Eagle screeched before rubbing its head against his face. Her wings were golden and feathery soft against his cheek. He was glad her arm was healed enough for her to shift

again. Just as he cursed himself for not being mindful of her injury when he ravished
her in his truck.

Otto felt his bear pushing to be let out.
Eager to meet his mate in animal form.
Otto fought back the urge to shift. He took a
deep breath and held it for a moment. As if
sensing his unease, Raya's Eagle flew away.
A minute later, Raya emerged from behind
his truck naked.

"Sorry, I tried not to shift, but my eagle
is stubborn," she blushed, sweeping her
discarded clothes off the ground.

Otto smirked. Maybe they weren't a lost
cause. If her Eagle couldn't be kept from
meeting him, perhaps the feelings he felt
weren't as one-sided as he thought.

"Yeah, my bear has been pushy to meet
you as well," he said.

Raya seemed stunned by the admission,
but she shook it off.

"Can we get inside? It's cold."

Her words instantly brought out his
protective side. He grabbed her and picked
her up, cradling her close to his body.

"Better," he breathed.

She swallowed and nodded. Otto

smiled, noticing the way her dark brown nipples puckered into tight peaks. His tongue flicked out as if to taste one, but he kept his tongue to himself for the time be-ing. He needed to exercise some restraint if they were ever going to have the talk they so desperately needed to have.

RAYA

Raya buried her face in Otto's chest as he carried her to his home, embarrassed. She shouldn't have been surprised to see the grand lodge in the clearing instead of the entrance to some dark cave. How ignorant was she really to think he actually lived in a fucking cave? Granted, the lodge wasn't his home. She snuck a peek and saw a cute little storybook cottage complete with wrap-around porch and his and hers red rocking chairs.

The inside was even worse. The outside was traditional, but the inside had a modern open concept with a giant fluffy couch that faced a massive stone fireplace and a gourmet kitchen. There were comfy throw blankets and color-coordinated throw pillows. There was a wide hallway that most likely led to the bedrooms.

It looked so unlike Otto but very much his style all at once. He would be the guy to build a place that would be his forever home. The kind of place that was ready-made for a wife and a few rambunctious cubs. Everything she couldn't give him. The thought was enough to temper the arousal that had lingered since their moment in the truck.

As soon as Otto kicked the door closed behind them, Raya wiggled out of his grasp. He set her down gently but didn't let her go. He held her flush against him, the rough cotton of his shirt rubbing against her nipples as he breathed. She pressed her hands against his chest, forcing space between them.

"Otto," she said barely above a whisper.

She kept her eyes at chest level, studying the patch of brown hair that peeked out of his partially unbuttoned shirt. She couldn't resist letting her fingers slide through the soft curls even as she avoided making eye contact.

"There is a second bedroom down the hall, first door on the left."

Otto took a step back and shoved her luggage between them. She dared a glance and noticed he too was avoiding looking at her. She hated the sharp bite of rejection she felt as he quickly put distance between them. Marching to the kitchen, Otto began fussing with the cupboards. Raya sighed and went to find the guest room.

OTTO

Coward!

Otto's bear was pissed. Their mate had been naked in their arms. Was now in their home, and he'd sent her to a room other than his own. Otto tried to reason that he was a good host. He shouldn't assume that just because they had slept together, she would want to share his bed for the duration of her stay with him. It was a hope and probably inevitable that she would move into his room, but he wouldn't force it on her.

Raya wasn't the kind of woman who responded well to being told what to do. Instead, he needed to play it safe. Starting with making a relaxing cup of tea. Anything to keep his hands busy and his mind off the fact that Raya was naked in the next room.

He filled the kettle with water and tried not to compare its weight with that of Raya's breasts. He started the flame on the stove and tried not to imagine the flash of warmth he felt whenever he and Raya were in the same room. When the kettle began to sweat, Otto's mind immediately jumped to the image of sweat running over her curves as she rode him with abandon. Then the water boiled, and the kettle whistled. Otto shut the flame off and moved the kettle before his mind thought of another kind of high-pitched scream.

So much for keeping his mind off Raya. He went to the cabinet to pull down two mugs. She hadn't returned from the room, and he wasn't sure that she would. He would be prepared either way.

Go to her!

Otto shook his head. He wanted to, but maybe she was already sleeping. Today had been a rough day. Perhaps, she needed some time to herself after being accosted by Vampires.

Go to her!

His body moved before his brain caught up. His bear took control, forcing him to the guest room. Otto got himself under control as he reached the door. He could quickly turn away and go back to his tea. He hesitated only a second too long.

"I can see your shadow!" Raya called from the other side of the door.

Otto cleared his throat.

"Sorry, I just wanted to ask if you would like some tea before bed."

There was shuffling. Then the door clicked open. Raya poked her head out and frowned at him.

"What kind of tea?"

Her hair was braided into a crown around her head, and she had changed into a silky pink pajama set. A thin camisole and shorts hugged her curves beneath a flowing robe with fake feathers around the collar. Her feet were bare and showed off a matching pink pedicure that he hadn't noticed before when she was naked in his arms. Otto licked his lips and forced his hands into his pockets to keep from reaching for her.

"Um, peppermint? Or chamomile?"

She made a face, and he was sure she was going to say no and slam the door in his face. Instead, she sighed and slid out of the room. She hooked her arm in his and smiled at him.

"A little chamomile won't hurt after the

day I had. Thank you."

They walked with arms linked down the short hall. She let go of him when they reached the kitchen and leaned against the butcher block island as he fixed her tea.

"Honey?"

"Did you harvest it yourself?"

Otto turned to look at her, and she laughed.

"You know, because bears love honey!"

He shook his head.

"I did not harvest it. Although, the honey does come from a local bee farm."

He added a small spoonful to her cup and stirred before handing it to her. He brought his own cup over, staying on his side of the island. She took a sip of her tea. Otto couldn't help but watch as she closed her eyes and let out a satisfied sigh.

"Thank you for letting me stay with you," she said after a moment of them silently sipping tea.

"It's really no issue," he assured her.

She set her tea down and moved around the island. Her robe fell off her shoulder, exposing more of her honeyed skin.

"Why don't we move to the couch?" she

said.

Otto cleared his throat and took a step back. He was trying to be on his best behavior here, and she wasn't helping.

"Uh, sure."

Raya smiled innocently at him before making a show of walking to the couch. Her long legs on full display as she strutted. Shaking his head, Otto followed like a dog after a bone, or rather, a male after his mate. He made it a point to sit on the opposite side of the couch from her.

"So, as much as I'd love to continue our sexual relationship, I think we need to talk about a few things first," Otto said.

Raya rolled her eyes.

"Is that really what you want to do right now?"

She lowered her robe further and closed the distance between them. Otto wished he had more self-control, but the sweet vanilla sugar fragrance wafting from her skin was his undoing.

"Fuck, I need you," he growled.

<u>RAYA</u>

Not needing to be told twice, she reached between them and undid his belt buckle and jeans. He sprung free as soon as she finished.

"Gorgeous," she gasped, eying his unencumbered flesh.

Otto stroked himself, a cocky grin spreading across his face.

"Baby, keep talking like that and see how gorgeous he gets," he laughed before gripping her shorts and tearing them from her body.

"You're such an animal," she teased, grabbing his hand before he could shred her panties.

She kissed him, pressing herself tightly against his chest to allow room to slide her panties down her legs. She was careful not to lean too much on her injured arm. She barely got one leg out before Otto guided a condom over his thick bobbing shaft.

"You have no idea," he growled.

She nibbled his neck as she lowered herself onto him. Raya loved hearing his breath hitch when she was fully seated on him. So deliciously full, he stretched her in all the right places. They lingered in relative silence, enjoying the feel of their bodies connected so intimately. Yet somehow, it wasn't enough.

"I need to feel you," Raya gasped.

"Like this," Otto chuckled, rolling his hips. She clutched his shoulders, riding out the waves of pleasure he spawned.

"I need you naked, your skin and mine," she gasped, grinding against him.

He nipped her collarbone.

"Patience, love. We have all the time in the world."

She didn't have time to ponder his words as he picked up the pace with his hips. Her body bounced on top of his, creating a frenzy within her. She exploded a moment later in pleasure so intense she saw stars. Her Eagle clawed to the surface, forcing a partial shift. Her wing attempted to wrap around them both. Her talons erupted once more and gripped his shoulders, drawing blood. Raya did her best to stop the change. Despite her earlier shift, her arm wasn't fully healed. The pain of shifting while injured was dampening her orgasmic bliss.

"Open your eyes, love," Otto demanded.

His deep, gravelly voice sounded harsher and more like a growl. Raya's eyes flew open, seeing him amid his own shift. She had no idea how a bear and a bird planned to fuck, but it seemed it was out of their control. They tumbled off the couch. Raya took advantage of the moment to position herself on top. The sight of his body hair thickening and turning to a furry pelt was intriguing, especially with her Eagle's vision allowing her to see everything so clearly.

Without warning, Otto's bear reared up and latched onto her shoulder. His bite tore into her flesh. She screamed as a hot burning desire ran from where he bit her to her core. She came again, this time harder than the first, and he was right behind her with a mighty roar. She collapsed on top of him, exhausted.

"Mate," Otto hummed, and tears formed in her eyes.

This was not how it was supposed to happen. This was not supposed to happen at all. So, while Raya's Eagle laid sated in mated bliss, Raya's brain attempted to plan an avenue of escape. She would undo this. To save both her and Otto the heartbreak when she couldn't be the mate he needed.

OTTO

Otto waited until Raya's breathing evened out before attempting to move. He may have marked her, but the connection between them was weak. She fought it, he knew. Otto saw it in her eyes when she realized what was happening. When their animals had forced a mating that shouldn't have occurred so soon. Raya would want to run, but he couldn't allow that. Not now. His bear would lose his shit if Otto let their mate go so quickly. Didn't try to win her love. The first step was to figure out what she was so afraid of.

He gently cradled her in his arms and carried her to bed. He didn't plan to hold Raya against her will. He just needed a chance to convince her to stay. To give him an honest to god chance.

The next morning, he awoke before she had a chance to slip away.

"Morning, love." He tried for light, but

the tension in her body spoke volumes.

She turned her golden-brown eyes on him, the flames of passion they once held now gone. Instead, he saw nothing but fear, and that hurt him deeply.

"You did this on purpose," she said, and he shook his head.

"I knew you were my mate, but I never meant to force it. I tried to stop him."

"You didn't try hard enough," she snapped.

Raya obviously blamed this all on him, but mating was a two-way street.

"Yeah, and neither did you, sweet cheeks."

He showed her where her claw marks still marred his chest. She bit her lip and turned away from him.

"This wasn't supposed to happen," she groaned.

"Let's start the day. I'll feed you, then we can get cleaned up." Otto got out of bed before she could protest.

She said nothing as he helped her into her robe, careful of her injured arm. He was such an ass for not noticing it earlier and taking special care with her. He took small comfort that she wasn't shying away from his touch. In fact, she leaned into him as he walked with her into the kitchen.

Once there, she turned in his arms and kissed his chin.

"I can't be your mate, Otto. We're too different."

Her words felt like a knife to his heart.

"So, you can fuck a bear but not mate one?"

"It's not that. I mean, it is but not entirely. I'm a city girl. I don't think I could adjust to being so deprived out here in the middle of nowhere. I couldn't ask you to leave your Sleuth for me no more than I could stay. Besides, as badass as my Eagle is, she wouldn't be the best match against any jealous bears that want a place at your side."

Otto laughed.

"Birdy, my place is only an hour from town and thirty minutes from your best friend. You think 24-hour stores are worth more than being with the ones you love?"

She pulled out of his arms. Biting her lip, she looked around his cabin.

"I won't fight for you. That's not in my

nature."

"Looking for any excuse, I see—honestly, Raya. You are my mate. I've known it since the moment I first saw you. I can be a bit more patient but not much, especially now that you wear my mark. I can give you time; we can take things as slowly as you need, but one thing is for certain. You are mine."

OTTO

Otto did his best to give Raya space for the rest of the morning, but the silence in his truck on the ride back to the Langsmith Compound killed him.

Raya sat squeezed against the passenger door as if she wanted to get as far away from him as possible. Her eyes trained on the trees lining the road. He could tell she was deep in thought because she didn't even bother picking up her phone, which buzzed every few minutes in her purse.

He cleared his throat.

"So, are we going to tell Tyr and Coy?"

Raya glared at him.

"What for? They have enough on their plates as it is. Whatever we are doing here isn't important."

"Not important?"

"You know what I mean."

"Yeah, I do," Otto huffed.

Raya rolled her eyes and reached over

to turn on the radio. Otto gripped the steering wheel tighter and pressed on the gas. He was pissed, and the need to shift rode him hard. He needed to get to Tyr's before he lost it and said or did anything else to push Raya further away.

Raya was out of the truck as soon as he parked in front of Tyr and Sequoia's cabin. He honestly couldn't blame her with how riled up he and his bear had gotten. She slammed the truck door hard and took off into the cabin before Otto even had the truck turned off.

Tyr bounded out of the cabin almost immediately and got in the truck with him.

"Holy fuck, man! What did you do?"

Otto sat there a moment, taking a few calming breaths before speaking.

"Things got complicated last night."

"No, shit!" Tyr chuckled. "Look, Coy tried to give me the run around at first. Just try to be patient."

"I mated her without asking!" Otto hissed.

Tyr glared at him before shaking his head.

"Fuck! I thought because you are

marked too…"

"Like I said, last night got complicated. Our animals took matters into their own hands."

"Man, you are screwed," Tyr said.

Otto nodded.

"Look, let's get things settled with the Shifter Council and how we are going to handle the Vampires. That's more important than my relationship screw up," Otto said.

Tyr nodded, and they both got out of the truck.

"We are doing a sweep of the area, breaking off into teams. One outsider, one local."

"Great, who am I paired with?" Otto asked.

"That would be me," Ward Buteo said, stepping out of the guest cabins followed by the rest of the Shifter Council.

Otto glared at Tyr, who shrugged and kept walking. Raya and Sequoia joined them, as well as Sarah, Tyr, and Sequoia's adopted daughter. There were a few others from Tyr's pack who joined the group. Reign, who was fresh out of seclusion and apparently freshly mated. Evidenced by the possessive grip he held on the strange woman by his side.

"Who is that?" Otto couldn't help but ask. There was something off about the woman. She made his bear tense up and his skin crawl.

Tyr smirked.

"The latest addition to the Greywulf pack. I'll explain later."

When Sequoia brought Raya to the woman, Otto immediately moved to Raya's side. To her credit, Raya only gave him a warning look but didn't shy away from his touch as he wrapped a protective arm around her.

"Otto, Raya. Meet Renata, Reign's mate."

"Nice to meet you, Renata." Raya extended her hand for the woman to shake but, after a moment, dropped it.

"Sorry, I don't mean to be rude. I just don't like being touched," Renata said.

"No worries."

Raya was much more diplomatic about the situation than Otto. His bear wanted to challenge Reign for his mate's slight to Raya. Reign must have sensed his animosity as he pulled Renata behind him.

"We should join the others and get this search underway," Sequoia said, breaking the tension as she pulled Raya away.

Otto's attention immediately focused on the loss of Raya in his arms. Still, by the time they had reached the rest of the group, sectors were already assigned, and Ward Buteo waited on him to get to work.

RAYA

Raya tried not to focus on Otto's ass as he strode away from her. She already gave up trying to fight the warm and fuzzies when he'd held her in his arms. There was nothing Raya could do about that. She was very attracted to the hairy beast. Hell, her bird had mated him already.

"Raya!" Sequoia snapped, bringing Raya's attention back to the moment.

"Sorry, where are we patrolling?"

Sequoia rolled her eyes.

"Tyr stuck us on the perimeter with Reign and Renata," she said.

It was Raya's turn to roll her eyes.

"Fine, let's not use the bird shifter to her full potential," she grumbled.

"I'd fuss more, but that means we won't take long and can hang out and talk about this mess you and Otto are in." Sequoia didn't give her a chance to reply before she shifted into her wolf.

Raya did the same, shifting into her Eagle, shaking off the stiffness in her wings before taking flight. A hawk swooped in next to her and screeched. Raya's Eagle climbed higher away from the intrusive Hawk, only for it to follow. It took her a minute to realize it must be Ward.

She settled into alignment with him as they circled Tyr and Sequoia's cabin. An angry roar sounded from below, drawing Raya's attention to Otto in bear form below them. She swooped down, batting the angry bear with her wings before taking off again. This time when he roared, she didn't look. She spotted Coy's black wolf and followed her through the trees away from the others.

OTTO

Otto wanted to take a large bite out of Ward Buteo when his Hawk swooped close to his head for the third time. The bastard was trying to control how they searched their section of the forest surrounding Langsmith. It would not happen. Otto knew precisely where he was going. He'd grown up in these parts, ran every inch countless times with Tyr and their friends.

When the Hawk swooped a fourth time, Otto's bear swiped at it. Catching the Hawk off guard, Otto's paw connected and sent it rolling through the dirt and leaves at his feet. Ward Buteo shifted back into human form, forcing Otto to do the same. It was bad enough he'd hit the guy. The last thing he wanted was for his bear to attack him in human form as well.

"What the fuck, Otto?"

"Sorry, my bear has been edgy with everything that's going on," Otto apologized half-heartedly.

"Yeah, well, if you are going to mate with a bird shifter, you both better learn to be more careful," Ward huffed.

"Going to? I already have, and trust me, Raya is well protected with me," he growled.

Ward shook his head.

"You better be sure of it. Any hint that Raya's unhappy, and I'll be right there to shit on your proverbial and literal windshield."

With that, Ward shifted back to his Hawk and took off, leaving Otto to stew over his words. At least, he didn't have to worry about the bird challenging him over Raya. Not that the man stood a chance against Otto if he did. Nothing would stand in the way of Otto and his mate. Especially, not now. He just needed to come up with a plan to convince her to stay.

RAYA

It only took two hours to circle the Langsmith Pack Territory twice, and after a quick shower, both women flopped on Sequoia's couch with glasses of red wine.

"Tell me what happened before the others get back?" Sequoia said.

Raya took a large sip of wine before setting her glass on the coffee table.

"Our animals got out of hand, and we mated without talking about it."

She waited for Sequoia's shock and horror, only to be disappointed when her best friend burst into a fit of laughter.

"I'm sorry, not really, but Jesus, Raya! Are you too that stubborn even your animals are tired of you two denying the obvious?"

Raya frowned.

"Coy! You know why this can't work."

"Yeah, you two aren't willing to compromise. I get it. It's scary to fall in love, but I gotta tell you I don't regret a single minute of being here with Tyr," Sequoia said.

"Yeah, but you were only up against other wolves. How the fuck am I supposed to fight a fucking bear?"

Shaking her head, Sequoia placed her hand on Raya's forehead like she was checking her temperature.

"You have already proven your status at the shifter gathering. No female is going to fight a fated mating. Not saying there aren't going to be females in his Sleuth that are pissed about you being their Alpha's choice, but if they were any competition, Otto had plenty of time to feel them out."

Raya didn't want Sequoia to be the rational one. She knew deep down that she was fighting the inevitable, but Raya wasn't one to back down from a fight, especially when it was her heart at stake.

"I'm exciting to him right now, but in a few months, years? He'll regret this. I'm sure."

Sequoia shook her head.

"Stop it! I know you're scared of settling down, but come on. Otto is the last man who would try to clip your wings. If you were just a curiosity to him, his bear never would have mated you."

Raya took a gulp of her wine and stared at the wall behind Sequoia's head. Was she scared? Hell yeah! Not saying that settling down had never crossed her mind, but Raya always assumed it would be with another free-spirited bird shifter. Someone she could travel with like Ward Buteo, not a bear stuck in the mountains with his Sleuth. At the thought of mating Ward, her Eagle screeched incredulously.

"You're right. I should just roll over and let the chips fall right," Raya sighed.

"Not exactly. I mean, I'm not telling you to give up on anything to be with Otto. All I'm saying is don't write him off just because you're scared. You two are cute together. I can tell you truly care for one another. Plus, I'm hoping you stick around just to be closer to me. I miss my best friend."

"I mean, sticking around wouldn't be too terrible. I mean, the sex with Otto is amazing. I wouldn't have to worry about kids with BB guns or clouds of smog in the mountains."

"See! Just give it a few months. Besides, I'm sure we will still need your help with this Vampire mess," Sequoia said.

"Perhaps." Raya wasn't entirely ready to commit just yet.

She needed to have a chat with Otto first before things got any more out of hand.

OTTO

Once their assigned grid was cleared, Otto and Ward headed back to the Langsmith Compound. They were skirting the main road when Otto's bear picked up on a strange scent. He turned toward it, bringing him deeper into the woods. Ward swooped low, letting Otto know he was following. They were traveling through someone else's search grid, and it wasn't long before they found whose it was.

Otto shifted back to human as soon as he spotted the two wolf shifters. They shifted as well.

"You smell that?" Otto asked in a hushed whisper.

The wolves nodded before shifting back to their animals and taking off toward the smell. Otto trailed the wolves, hanging back a few yards. The scent of fresh blood grew stronger and stronger until they came upon the source. A Vampire sat on his haunches over the body of a young woman.

The wolves didn't wait before lunging forward to attack. Ward screeched in warning, but it was too late. Four more Vampires rushed in carrying automatic weapons. Bullets flew, the two wolves caught in the crossfire. Otto charged the nearest Vampire. He managed to stop two before the first bullet pierced his flesh.

He roared in pain and anger before whirling on his shooter. He took the man out during the brief period he paused to reload his weapon. One wolf was still standing and got the last Vampire, latching onto its throat and snapping it with a sickening crunch.

The woman in the clearing sat wide-eyed and afraid. Tears streamed down her face, and she reeked of fear. She was human. Otto approached slowly and nudged her with his nose. She scrambled away from him, but Otto tried again.

He couldn't shift back to human. It would take too much of his already waning energy and expose the secret of shifters to the human. Finally, she understood he wasn't a threat. He grunted and nudged her toward his back. She nodded and stood slowly before gripping his fur. Otto guided the woman to the main road while Ward circled overhead.

At the side of the road, Otto recognized Donovan Mars and his mate Farrah leaning against a black SUV.

"We've got her from here," Donovan said to Otto.

Farrah had already come to the woman's side and guided her to the car. Otto felt the calming energy pulsing from Farrah and had to fight the urge to collapse on the side of the road. He pushed himself back into the treeline and away from the Aura couple.

He needed to make it back to the compound to report in. The Vampires had set up this ambush in the middle of shifter territory. There was no telling what else they had planned. Fear welled in his heart, thinking of Raya and Coy caught in a similar trap. That fear was the fuel he needed to make it back to the compound. He didn't even bother shifting to human. He followed Raya's scent to Tyr and Sequoia's cabin and let out a low growl.

His heart skipped a beat when Raya ran

out of the cabin.

"Otto! Holy Shit! What happened?"

He tried to shift back so he could answer her, but exhaustion overcame him, and the world faded around him. The last thing he saw— the concerned look on Raya's face.

RAYA

"Otto! Otto!"

Raya sat, shaking the unconscious bear in front of her. Tears streamed down her face as her hands frantically tried to find where all the blood matting his fur came from.

"Raya, please, we need to take him to the infirmary."

Sequoia's voice barely registered. Raya was too distraught over the possibility of losing her mate.

"Raya, let us help him."

This time it wasn't a gentle suggestion but an Alpha's command. Not being an Alpha, Raya couldn't fight the instinct to obey. She slowly pushed away from the ground as four men crowded around to pick Otto up. Sequoia was right there, drawing her into a hug.

"Shh, it's okay. He's going to be okay."

No longer holding Otto, Raya's concern

quickly morphed to anger. She pulled out of her friend's grasp. Searching the gathered crowd, Raya's eyes landed on the perfect target for her rage. She marched to Ward and shoved him as hard as she could.

"What did you do to him? Why did you let this happen?"

She yelled and shoved him, an Alpha, a Shifter Council member, but she couldn't have cared less. Ward had been paired with Otto, and there wasn't a scratch on him.

Ward let her shove him a few more times before he grabbed her shoulders and held her at bay. Looking into her eyes, he seemed to stare deep into her soul.

"Who do you think alerted the others to bring help? To be prepared to tend to our injured brothers and sisters? I won't hold your angry outburst against you this time, but get yourself together. You need to be strong for your mate."

With that, he let her go. Raya hadn't realized he'd been holding her up until she nearly crumpled to the ground. This time, Sarah was with Sequoia as she fell into their waiting arms. The two women guided her into the cabin.

Time seemed to stand still for Raya. Her mind raced with every worst-case scenario imaginable. Sequoia and Sarah brought her a blanket and snacks, only checking in to make sure she had at least nibbled on something.

How could I miss how much that stupid bear meant to me?

Please, God let Otto live! I know I've been mean to him. That I have denied my feelings for him. I apologize for being blinded by my selfishness. I can't lose him. He's my mate!

Raya wallowed in her shock and grief for hours before Tyr came into the living room.

"You can see him now. We were able to get him to shift back to human form, but he'll have to stay in the infirmary overnight."

Tyr barely finished his sentence before Raya rushed for the door. She ran for the infirmary, not caring who she pushed out of the way to get there. Her heart nearly broke seeing Otto's patched up body, lying pale and still on the bed. She went to him and took his hand in hers. His skin felt clammy and cold, but then his head slowly turned, and his eyes fluttered open.

"Hey, Birdy," he said weakly.

Raya laughed, tears of happiness streaming down her face. She bent over and pressed a kiss to his forehead.

"You reckless jackass. You did this on purpose, knowing I couldn't possibly leave," she whispered.

Otto smirked.

"Right. I got myself shot to hell, just so you would have to baby me like a toddler for a few weeks. Like that is so much better than tying you to my bed and making love to you until you couldn't think, let alone walk your fine ass out the door."

"Oh, you can definitely try that, but later, after you're all healed."

Otto's face turned serious.

"Raya, you don't have to stay just because I got hurt. I mean, I hope you stay but not for that reason."

It was Raya's turn to laugh.

"I'm staying because someone has to look after you, because Sequoia needs me too, but most importantly because I love you, Otto."

Otto grabbed her hand and pulled her

on top of him.

"Repeat it," he growled.

Raya shook her head and tried to move off of him, but he held her tighter.

"I don't want you busting any stitches," she said.

"Just say it again," he said.

"Not until you say it first."

Otto chuckled, wincing before he covered her mouth with his. His tongue danced along the seam of her lips before pulling away.

"I love you, Raya. I have since the moment I saw you at the Shifter Gathering."

"Liar."

"I swear on my Sleuth. I was a goner from day one, and I have a feeling you were too."

"I honestly don't know when exactly I fell so hard for you, but does it really matter?"

Otto shook his head and kissed her again.

"Not as long as you do."

More from Stella Williams

www.serpentinecreative.com/getbooks

<u>**Maura's Men Trilogy**</u>
Hot Vampire Loving and diabolical villain you can't help but to love.

Xander's Claim
Interracial BWWM Vampire Romance
Claude's Conquest
A sinful seduction tale.
Shane's Redemption
Redemption comes in many forms.
Maura's Men Complete Trilogy
Additional Villain Origins Short

<u>**Secret of Ceres Series**</u>
Black Girl Magic and Steamy Black Love

Ferocious
Mystery, intrigue and sexy self-gratification,
Dauntless
The personal and professional collide in this ex lovers tale.
Earnest
Death and daring feats await in this tale of forbidden love.

<u>**Langsmith Shifters**</u>
Alpha Shifters Shorts

Coy Wolf
Alpha Wolf Shifters
A Night Divine
Mardi Gras Themed Fun.
Bird of Prey

A Sexy Eagle Shifter meets her match.

About the Author

Stella Williams is a Blogger and Romance Author, who lives in Washington State. She has a degree in Anthropology from The University of California, Santa Cruz. Stella prides herself in using her studies to create diverse worlds and characters for her novels.

You can find more about Stella at her website www.serpentinecreative.com.

Keep up to date with Stella Williams' latest projects.

Join Our Mailing List

https://mailchi.mp/2637cc1d4d12/getcreative